b. 30726219

INVESTIGATING
SCIENCE
CHALLENGES

Investigating ELECTRICITY

Richard Spilsbury

CRABTREE
PUBLISHING COMPANY
WWW.CRABTREEBOOKS.COM

CRABTREE
PUBLISHING COMPANY
WWW.CRABTREEBOOKS.COM

Author: Richard Spilsbury

Editors: Sarah Eason, Jennifer Sanderson, Petrice Custance, Reagan Miller

Proofreaders: Kris Hirschmann, Janine Deschenes

Indexer: Harriet McGregor

Editorial director: Kathy Middleton

Design: Emma DeBanks

Cover design and additional artwork: Emma DeBanks

Photo research: Rachel Blount

Production coordinator and prepress technician: Tammy McGarr

Print coordinator: Katherine Berti

Consultant: David Hawksett

Produced for Crabtree Publishing Company by Calcium Creative

Photo Credits:

t=Top, tr=Top Right, tl=Top Left

Inside: Shutterstock: ArtisticPhoto: p. 11b; Anton Balazh: p. 5t; Alfonso de Tomas: p. 6b; Dpaint: pp. 22-23; Peter Hermes Furian: p. 12; Gansstock: p. 13; v: p. 23r; Inked Pixels: pp. 20-21; Jakinnboaz: p. 15; Mandritoiu: pp. 4-5; MNStudio: p. 19; Mohamadhafizmohamad: p. 18; Daniel Prudek: pp. 10-11; Scharfsinn: pp. 1, 27t; Science Photo: pp. 26-27; Vladyslav Starozhylov: p. 20; Suwan Waenlor: p. 14; Wesley West: pp. 6-7.

Cover: Tudor Photography.

Library and Archives Canada Cataloguing in Publication

Spilsbury, Richard, 1963-, author
    Investigating electricity / Richard Spilsbury.

(Investigating science challenges)
Includes index.
Issued in print and electronic formats.
ISBN 978-0-7787-4183-1 (hardcover).--
ISBN 978-0-7787-4210-4 (softcover).--
ISBN 978-1-4271-2008-3 (HTML)

    1. Electricity--Juvenile literature. 2. Physics--Juvenile literature.
I. Title.

QC527.2.S66 2018   j537   C2017-907734-1
                             C2017-907735-X

Library of Congress Cataloging-in-Publication Data

Names: Spilsbury, Richard, 1963- author.
Title: Investigating electricity / Richard Spilsbury.
Description: New York, New York : Crabtree Publishing, [2018] |
Series: Investigating science challenges | Audience: Ages 8-11. |
    Audience: Grades 4 to 6. | Includes index.
Identifiers: LCCN 2017057531 (print) | LCCN 2017059305 (ebook) |
    ISBN 9781427120083 (Electronic HTML) |
    ISBN 9780778741831 (reinforced library binding : alk. paper) |
    ISBN 9780778742104 (pbk. : alk. paper)
Subjects: LCSH: Electricity--Juvenile literature. | Physics--Juvenile
    literature.
Classification: LCC QC527.2 (ebook) | LCC QC527.2 .S664194 2018
    (print) | DDC 537--dc23
LC record available at https://lccn.loc.gov/2017057531

Crabtree Publishing Company
www.crabtreebooks.com   1-800-387-7650

Printed in the U.S.A./022018/CG20171220

Published in Canada
Crabtree Publishing
616 Welland Ave.
St. Catharines, Ontario
L2M 5V6

Published in the United States
Crabtree Publishing
PMB 59051
350 Fifth Avenue, 59th Floor
New York, New York 10118

Published in the United Kingdom
Crabtree Publishing
Maritime House
Basin Road North, Hove
BN41 1WR

Published in Australia
Crabtree Publishing
3 Charles Street
Coburg North
VIC, 3058

CONTENTS

ELECTRICAL ENERGY

We flick a switch to turn on a lamp, watch television, play music, and power a toaster. These machines work as soon as we turn them on because of electricity. It is hard to imagine how different our lives would be without electricity. We only realize how much we rely on electrical energy when there is a power outage and cities and homes are plunged into darkness.

What Is Energy?

Energy is the ability to make things move, work, or happen. Electrical energy is just one type of energy. Sound, light, heat, and kinetic, or movement, are other types of energy. We get electrical energy in different ways. **Batteries** supply electrical energy to cell phones and we plug many machines, including televisions, DVD players, and computers, into wall sockets to get the electricity we need to make them work. Electricity also powers the **motors** that make many cars, buses, trains, and boats move.

The electricity we use to power most of the machines in our homes, schools, and workplaces comes from **power plants**. It travels from a power plant through cables to our homes. We access this energy when we plug our machines into wall sockets and turn them on.

Can you imagine what life was like before people had electricity? What would this picture look like if someone turned off the power?

INVESTIGATE

Scientists **observe** the world around them and ask questions. They then plan and carry out **investigations** to find answers. In this book, you will carry out investigations to answer questions about electricity. On pages 28 and 29 you can find investigation tips, check your work, and read suggestions for other investigations you can try.

HOW ELECTRICITY HAPPENS

Electrical energy can do big things, such as light up a city, but electricity happens at the tiny, invisible level of **atoms**. All matter is made up of tiny particles called atoms. Atoms are made up of even smaller parts called **protons, electrons,** and **neutrons**. Protons and neutrons form the center of an atom and they do not move. Electrons move around the center of an atom incredibly quickly.

Charge

Neutrons have no **charge** of electricity: they are neither positive nor negative. Protons have a positive charge and electrons have a negative charge. Usually, an atom has an equal number of protons and electrons. Their positive and negative charges balance, so the atom has no overall electrical charge. Electricity is created when electrons escape from one atom, move, and join another atom, giving that atom a negative charge.

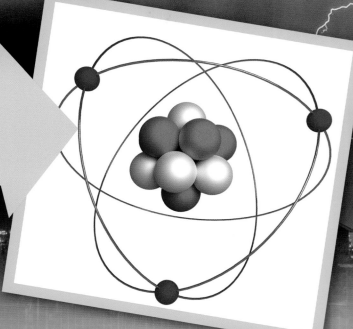

This model of an atom is not to scale, but it gives you an idea of how the protons and neutrons in the atom's center are surrounded by moving electrons.

6

Static Electricity

Have you ever rubbed a balloon on your hair to make your hair stand on end? This happens because of **static electricity**. Static electricity is when electrons shift so charges build up in an object. This can happen when surfaces, such as a balloon and your hair, rub together. Some electrons move from atoms in your hair to the atoms in the balloon. Then the balloon has a slight negative charge and your hair has a slight positive charge. Opposite charges attract, and your hair is lightweight enough to be pulled or attracted toward the balloon by static electricity. The tiny charges involved would not be strong enough to pull a heavier weight.

Lightning is an example of powerful static electricity. It happens when tiny pieces of ice blow around inside a cloud. As ice rubs together, electrons shift between atoms. When enough static electricity builds up, it can jump from the cloud, creating a bolt of lightning.

INVESTIGATE

Have you ever felt a slight shock when you jump on a trampoline, walk on a carpet, or touch a doorknob? This happens because these and many other kinds of objects can store static electricity. What happens to make you feel a shock? Touch different materials in your home to see if any give you a shock. Would it be different after rubbing an inflated balloon on them? Why do you think this is? Decide what you think will happen, then try it out!

STATIC CHALLENGE

The pulling **force** of attraction between objects with different static electrical charges can be strong enough to cause one object to stick to another. Do you think that the force could make them move together? Let's investigate how static electricity works.

THINK!

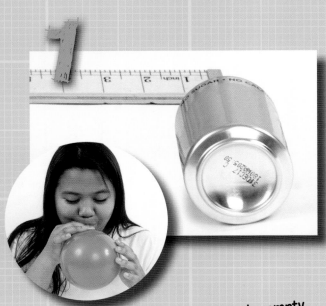

Step 1: Blow up the balloon. Put the empty soda can on its side on a flat surface. Put the yardstick, meterstick, or ruler on the flat surface with the zero in line with the center of the front of the can.

Step 2: Rub the balloon back and forth quickly through your hair for about 30 seconds.

Step 3: Move the balloon close to the can, but it must not touch it. When the balloon gets close enough, the can should start to roll toward it. Measure the distance between the can and the balloon when movement starts. Write down the measurement.

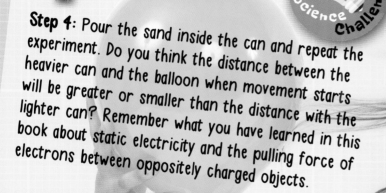

Step 4: Pour the sand inside the can and repeat the experiment. Do you think the distance between the heavier can and the balloon when movement starts will be greater or smaller than the distance with the lighter can? Remember what you have learned in this book about static electricity and the pulling force of electrons between oppositely charged objects.

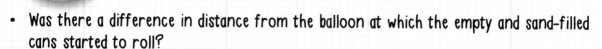

- Was there a difference in distance from the balloon at which the empty and sand-filled cans started to roll?
- If there was, how did the sand inside the can make a difference to the static electricity?
- Why is it important to use the same can and balloon and start them in the same position in all the tests?

9

FLOWING ELECTRICITY

When we flick a switch to turn on an electrical machine, we use **current** electricity. This form of electricity is very useful because it moves or flows in a current to carry electrical energy from one place to another. The current we use is made in power plants and travels to where we need it.

Energy can never be made or destroyed, but it can be changed from one form to another. Power plants change energy several times to make electrical energy.

Creating Currents

Power plants create electric currents by converting the energy stored in a **source**, such as coal or natural gas, into electrical energy. Machines in power plants can do this because energy is never destroyed, but it can change, again and again, from one form to another. Some power plants burn coal to change the chemical energy stored inside it into heat energy. The heat energy is used to boil water and make steam. The steam hits the blades of a **turbine**, which is like a big fan, making the turbine spin. This turns the heat energy into kinetic, or movement, energy. The spinning turbine turns coils of wire past large magnets in a **generator**. These magnets create strong pulling forces and as the wires spin between the magnets, electrons in the wire are forced to move between atoms. Kinetic energy has turned into electrical energy and an electric current starts to flow through the wire.

Pass It On

A current keeps flowing because all atoms want to have the same number of protons and electrons. Atoms that lose electrons attract more electrons from atoms around them. This sets off a chain reaction. As an atom loses an electron, it takes one from another atom, leaving that atom short of electrons. That one steals an electron from yet another atom, and so on, and so on. When electrons move, the current can flow through wires in an electrical system.

An electric current can move through wires all the way from a power plant to our homes and other buildings.

CONDUCTORS AND INSULATORS

Electrical energy in currents flows through some materials more easily than others. People use metal wires to carry electric currents from power plants across long distances to homes, schools, and other buildings because metal is a good **conductor**. Conductors are materials that allow electron charges to flow through them easily. Materials that do not conduct electron charges well are called **insulators**. Electrical insulators are the opposite of electrical conductors.

Copper is used to make electric wires because copper conducts electricity quickly and efficiently.

Metal wires are covered in plastic insulators. Circular ceramic insulators stop electric currents from flowing down metal pylons.

Conductors in Action

Most of the materials that are good at conducting electricity are metal, but some metals are better conductors than others. For example, aluminum is a poor conductor but electrons flow very easily through copper. This is why copper is one of the metals most commonly used in electric cables and wires. Some other materials, such as water, are poor conductors but electricity can still flow through them. This is why it is very important to make sure your hands are completely dry before you touch anything electrical. If water conducts electricity into your body, it can cause an **electric shock** that can badly burn or even kill you.

Insulators at Work

An electric charge cannot flow through an insulating material, so insulators are used to stop the flow of electricity. Insulators can stop electricity from being wasted or hurting somebody. The metal wires that carry an electric current from a wall socket into your computer or lamp are usually covered in plastic, because plastic is a good insulator. The plastic insulation on wires, plugs, and wall sockets prevents electric shocks. Other electrical insulators include glass, rubber, dry cloth, and ceramics that are made from clay hardened by heat.

13

WHAT IS A CIRCUIT?

An electrical **circuit** is a path that an electric current flows through. Electricity can flow only if it has a complete loop, or circuit, of wires through which the current can move. If a racecar driver on a circular race track meets a barrier halfway around the track, they can drive no farther. An electric current also needs a continuous path through which to flow, in order to keep moving. If a circuit is incomplete, electricity cannot flow.

The Parts of a Circuit

The parts needed for a basic circuit include a power source, from which the electric current comes. A power source could inlude a wall socket or batteries. Circuits also need a conductor, the metal wires that carry electricity from place to place. The wires carry the current to the **load**, or the object that is being powered, such as a bulb or computer. Another important part of a circuit is the switch. This connects the circuit and starts the electricity flowing to the load. A switch makes or breaks the circuit to turn the load on or off.

Switches are very useful because they allow us to control an electric circuit. We can turn off machines when they are not in use.

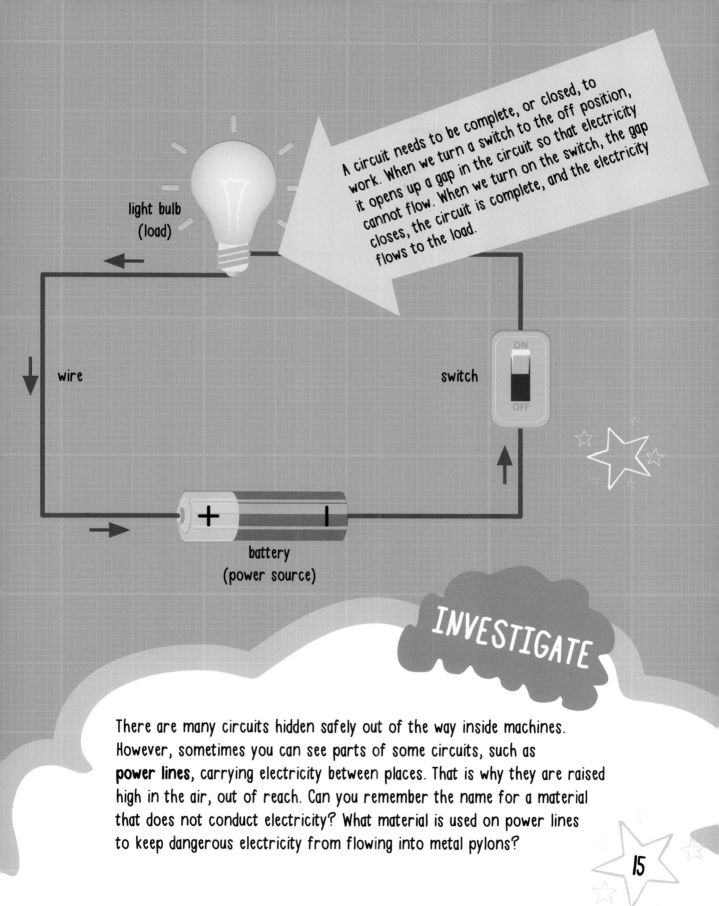

light bulb
(load)

A circuit needs to be complete, or closed, to work. When we turn a switch to the off position, it opens up a gap in the circuit so that electricity cannot flow. When we turn on the switch, the gap closes, the circuit is complete, and the electricity flows to the load.

wire

switch

ON

OFF

battery
(power source)

INVESTIGATE

There are many circuits hidden safely out of the way inside machines. However, sometimes you can see parts of some circuits, such as **power lines**, carrying electricity between places. That is why they are raised high in the air, out of reach. Can you remember the name for a material that does not conduct electricity? What material is used on power lines to keep dangerous electricity from flowing into metal pylons?

Let's Investigate

ON THE CIRCUIT

You Will Need:
- 5 aluminum foil strips about 0.6 inches (1.5 cm) wide
- 2 sheets of paper
- A D-cell battery
- Tape
- A rubber band
- A 1.5-volt light bulb
- A clothespin
- Test materials including a paper clip, a cork, a lump of modeling clay, a matchstick, a nail, a plastic spoon, and a short pencil, sharpened at each end
- A pen
- An adult to help

Have you noticed which materials are used in circuits and which are not? It all comes down to insulators and conductors. Let's carefully investigate the conduction of different materials.

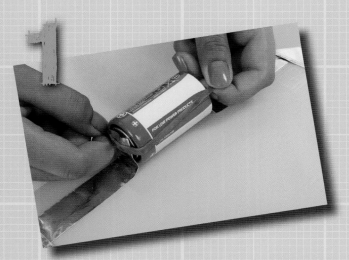

first strip

second strip

test leads

third strip

Step 1: Make 5 foil strips about 0.6 inches (1.5 cm) wide, by folding pieces of foil about 12 inches x 6 inches (30 cm × 15 cm) in half again and again. Construct the circuit on a sheet of paper as shown, using the foil strips instead of wires. Attach one strip securely to each end of the battery using tape and the rubber band. The other end of the first strip is called a test lead.

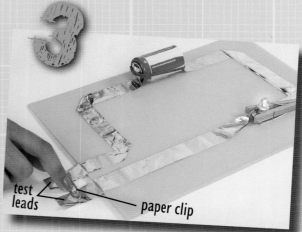

test leads — paper clip

Step 2: Use tape to connect the end of the second strip from the battery to the bottom of the bulb. Connect a third strip to the side of the bulb by clamping it in position with the clothespin. The other end of this strip is another test lead.

Step 3: Now place the paper clip so it touches both test lead ends. The paper clip is the test material. Write down what happens.

Step 4: Repeat the experiment several times using a different test material from the You Will Need list that will **not** complete the circuit. Remember what you have learned in this book about conductors and insulators. Which types of materials prevent the flow of current?

Science Challenge

Challenge Questions

- Why did the light bulb glow when some materials bridged the test leads but did not glow when other materials were used?
- What materials did you choose to break the circuit and why?
- Why do you think aluminum foil was used to make your circuit?

17

HEAT AND LIGHT

Electrical energy is very useful because it can move through wires to places where it can easily be changed into other forms of energy to carry out different tasks. For example, when we burn wood, some of the chemical energy stored in that **fuel** turns into light energy and some turns into heat energy. We use electrical energy in our everyday lives by converting it into light or heat energy to help us see, keep us warm, and cook our food.

Feel the Heat!

Electric ovens, hair dryers, toasters, and heaters change electrical energy into heat energy using **resistance**. Resistance is how well a material prevents, or resists, the flow of a current of electricity. Like insulators, resistant materials are made up of atoms that hold their electrons very tightly. For example, a toaster has long lengths of wire made of high-resistance metal curled into loops. These slow down the electric current flowing through them and when this happens, some of the electrical energy is converted into heat. The wires glow with heat (and light) to toast the bread.

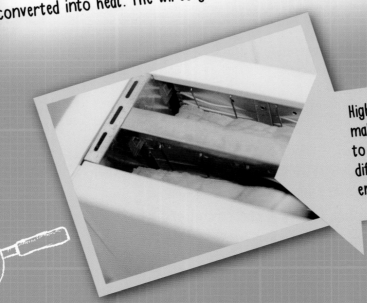

High-resistance wires in a toaster make it harder for the electricity to move. When the electricity has difficulty traveling, it releases heat energy from the wires.

18

All Lit Up

Lights help us see and keep us safe every day. As soon as it gets dark outside, we turn on lamps. Computers and television screens change electrical energy into light so we can see the images on their screens. Some light bulbs have wires inside connected by a length of thin wire coiled up like a tight spring, called a filament. Together, these wires form part of the circuit. As electrons flow through the filament, the filament becomes hotter and hotter until it glows white hot and gives off light.

When you squeeze a hose, it causes resistance that slows or stops the flow of water in it. Something similar happens with electrical wire. Longer, thinner wires create more resistance than shorter, wider wires because it takes electrons longer to move through them.

MOVING WITH ELECTRICITY

The energy in electric currents can also be used to produce movement. Many of the things we use every day have electric motors. Motors are machines that convert electrical energy into kinetic energy. There are motors in ceiling fans, hair dryers, washing machines, buses, cars, and the robots we call drones. Motors rely on the effect that a current has on the wire it moves through. The current turns the wire into a magnet.

A hoverboard is powered by a large battery, which provides the electricity needed to power the motors for the wheels. Riders control the speed by leaning forward or backward, and change direction by twisting the pads they stand on.

How Motors Work

When electrical energy runs through a wire, it creates an invisible force of energy all around it called a **magnetic field**. Coiling a wire makes the magnetic field stronger. The magnetic force disappears when the current is switched off and changes depending on which way the current is running through the wire. An electric motor has a magnet inside an **electromagnet**. An electromagnet is a magnet that is created and controlled by the flow of electricity. The two magnetic fields push and pull against each other in the motor when power is switched on. This makes the electromagnet spin around the magnet.

Motorized Machines

All motorized machines use an electric motor to produce kinetic energy. For example, a washing machine spins slowly to clean clothing and spins fast to remove excess water. Other useful spinning motions from electric motors include turning the wheels on a car, blowing air from a hair dryer, and sucking dust into a vacuum cleaner. In other machines, the spinning motion is converted into other movements. For example, a car's windshield wipers change circular movement into side-to-side motion to wipe raindrops off the glass.

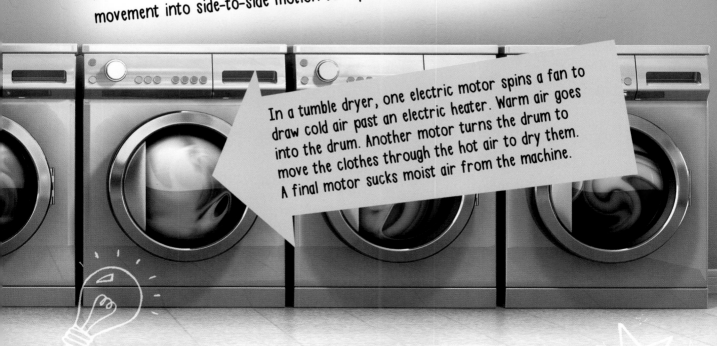

In a tumble dryer, one electric motor spins a fan to draw cold air past an electric heater. Warm air goes into the drum. Another motor turns the drum to move the clothes through the hot air to dry them. A final motor sucks moist air from the machine.

WIRED FOR SOUND

Electrical energy can also be converted into sound energy, and sound energy can be converted into electrical energy using machines. To capture a sound, people can use **microphones**.

What Is Sound?

A sound starts with the **vibration** of an object, such as a plucked guitar string. When any object vibrates, it makes the air around it vibrate. The vibrations are passed on through air as **sound waves**. Inside a microphone there is a thin, stretched layer that vibrates as the sound waves hit it. This makes a coil of wire vibrate, too. The wire turns the patterns of kinetic energy into bursts of electricity called **electrical signals**. The signals can pass through wires to a loudspeaker, where the reverse process happens. Loudspeakers convert electrical energy into kinetic energy and then into sound energy.

Turn Up the Volume

An amplifier is a machine that turns small electrical signals into bigger ones, so people can hear sounds louder. The loudness, or volume, is controlled in the amplifier by changing a circuit. This circuit includes a loop of wire made of metal with high resistance. Turning a volume knob changes how much of this wire the electrical signal has to pass through. Making the current travel farther increases the resistance and makes the sound quieter. Reducing the distance makes the sound louder.

Music can be stored as files on computers or grooves on a vinyl disk until people want to play them. Then, turntables convert the stored information into electrical signals, which headphones and speakers change into sounds.

The **pickup** in an electric guitar is a metal bar containing magnets under the strings. It converts their vibrations into electrical signals, a little like the way a microphone works.

INVESTIGATE

Loudspeakers can produce dangerously loud sounds if the volume is turned up, so it is best to keep your distance. Have you ever been close enough to a loudspeaker to see the circular part (called the cone) inside vibrate when it is playing music? Can you figure out how this happens?

Let's Investigate

POWER TO CONES

An electric current is the flow of an electric charge. When electrical signals produced in a microphone flow as an electric current to a loudspeaker, they can make the cone in the loudspeaker move. These vibrations are how a loudspeaker produces sound waves and sounds. Let's investigate how a current produces sound by making loudspeaker cones from different materials.

You Will Need:

- About 24 inches (60 cm) of thin magnet wire
- A pencil
- Tape
- A paper cup
- 2 alligator-clip leads
- A pair of scissors
- An old set of earphones that you no longer need
- A music player, such as an MP3 player
- A circular magnet about 1 inch (2.5 cm) across
- A foam cup
- A ceramic cup or mug
- An adult to help

Step 1: Coil the magnet wire around the pencil leaving 4 inches (10 cm) free at each end. Slip the coil off the pencil and tape it to the outside of the bottom of the paper cup. Attach one end of each alligator clip to each wire end.

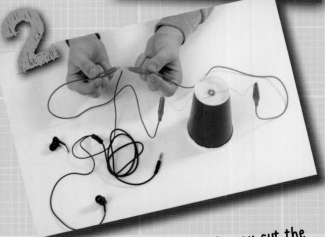

Step 2: Ask an adult to help you cut the ear pieces from the earphones. Scrape back the plastic to reveal the two wires inside the cable. Attach the other end of each alligator clip to one wire.

24

Step 3: Insert the earphone plug into the MP3 player's earphone socket. Turn on some music. With one hand, put the cup to your ear. With the other hand, hold the magnet next to the coil. The magnet helps the coil move in or out to make sounds louder. Can you hear sounds?

Science Challenge

Step 4: Now repeat steps 1 to 3. However, this time choose the foam cup and then the ceramic cup or mug to see what makes a sound as loud, or louder, than the paper cup. Remember what you have already learned in this book about how electrical signals moving through wires change into sound waves. What material do you think converts signals into sound best?

Challenge Questions

- Which cup made the loudest sound and which cup made the weakest sound?
- What types of material are best for making loudspeaker cones?
- What measures can you take to ensure that the investigation is accurate?

INVESTIGATE MORE

People use electricity almost every minute of their daily lives, from the moment they wake up until they turn off their lights at bedtime. Every day there are new electronic devices for people to choose from, and people are using more and more electricity.

Making Electricity

Most of the world's electricity is made by burning **fossil fuels**. Fossil fuels include coal, oil, and natural gas. These are **nonrenewable resources** because one day they will run out. Burning fossil fuels causes air pollution and releases gases into the air that trap more of the Sun's warmth on Earth. This process of **global warming** contributes to changing weather patterns. Changing weather patterns have an impact on industries such as farming, and increase extreme weather events such as droughts, floods, and hurricanes.

Using Less Electricity

The less electricity we use, the less pollution there will be—and it also saves us money. There are many ways to use less electricity. We can buy appliances that are designed to use less energy, such as energy-efficient light bulbs and washing machines. We can **insulate** our homes to stop heat from escaping through gaps around windows and doors, and forcing heaters to work harder to keep us warm. You can unplug appliances and chargers when not in use and take quicker showers to minimize the water heater's workload. What else could you do to save energy?

Electric cars need to be charged to work. However, they give off a lot less pollution than cars that burn fossil fuels, so they are less damaging to the environment.

Renewable Energy

Another way to reduce the amount of fossil fuels used is to make electricity from **renewable resources**. These are resources that will not run out and are in plentiful supply, such as blowing wind, rushing water, and light and heat from the Sun. We use **solar panels** and turbines to convert those energy sources into electrical energy. These types of energy also cause less damage to the environment.

Large solar-power plants can convert the Sun's heat and light energy into enough electricity to power whole towns, but people can also use solar energy to power small gadgets and devices.

INVESTIGATE

What machines and devices are used to convert renewable energy sources into flowing electrons? Investigate the environmental impacts of using renewable resources for power. How do renewable resources vary in different parts of Earth and at different times of day? What things can people do to ensure a steady supply of power? What other amazing sources of power can you find out about?

TIPS

Pages 8-9: Static Challenge

The distance between the balloon and the can should be smaller to move the sand-filled can than the empty can. Rubbing the balloon builds up a negative charge on the balloon's surface. The electrons want to move from the balloon to the can to even out the charges. So, when the balloon moves close to the can, it attracts the can. Adding sand to the can has no effect on the amount of static in the balloon, but the extra weight makes it more difficult for the negative charge to pull the can closer. By using the same can and balloon and starting them in the same position in all the tests, the investigation will be accurate and fair. You can try to figure out the exact weight of sand needed to prevent the balloon from moving the can. What effect do you think rubbing the balloon for longer would have on the outcome? Give reasons for your thinking.

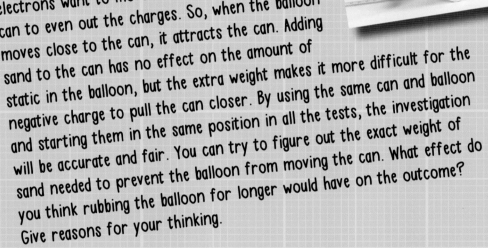

Pages 16-17 On the Circuit

You should find that the light bulb can glow only when the circuit is completed or closed with materials that are conductors. Of the test materials, the conductors include the nail, which is made from conducting metal, and the modeling clay. The clay contains water and salt that can conduct electricity. Wood, cork, and plastic are insulators that should break the circuit. You may find that the short pencil allows the bulb to glow, but dimly. That is because the pencil lead is made from a material called graphite that can conduct electricity, but not very well. Metals are good conductors, which is why aluminum works best for the circuit. Real electric wires usually contain copper. Find out more about why copper is used in electric wires and why it is not so safe to handle in electrical experiments such as this one.

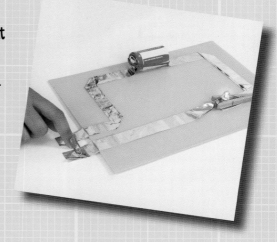

Note: The circuit in Step 3 might not work if the battery is low on power or dead, the bulb is broken, or if the conducting strips of aluminum are too thin or not properly connected to the battery or bulb.

Pages 24-25: Power to Cones

You should find that the paper cup and foam cups make the loudest sound and the ceramic cup the weakest. The transfer of electrical energy to sound energy happens at the cone of a loudspeaker. When electric signals move through wires from the MP3 player into the coil, they turn it into an electromagnet. This makes the coil move closer or farther from the ring magnet, making the bottom of the cup move in and out.

Paper and foam are lighter and more flexible, so these cups vibrate more than the ceramic cup. They make louder sound waves so they are better for making loudspeaker cones. Most loudspeakers have cones made from cardboard or thin plastic, often mounted on rubber rings. The rings make sure the vibrations of the cone, which are necessary for sound production, are not lost through the outer boxes of the loudspeaker. To make the test accurate, you should ensure that the volume is at the same level for each type of cone.

Note: You may need to turn up the volume on the MP3 player to hear anything through your homemade speaker in this investigation.

GLOSSARY

Some bold-faced words are defined
where they appear in the text.

atoms The tiny particles that make up everything. Atoms are so small that we cannot see them.

batteries Devices that convert stored chemical energy into electrical energy in a circuit

charge Having more (negative) or fewer (positive) electrons than protons

conductor A material or object that transfers heat and electrical energy well

current The flow of electrons from one place to another

electric shock A dangerous reaction in the body caused by an electric current running through it

electrical signals Patterns of electric currents

electromagnet A magnet created and controlled by the flow of electricity

electrons The very small parts of an atom that have a negative electric charge

energy Ability or power to do work

force The effect that causes things to move in a particular way, usually a push or a pull

fossil fuels Fuels, such as oil or coal, that formed under the ground from ancient fossils

fuel A material such as coal, gasoline, or oil that is burned to produce heat or power

generator A machine that makes electricity

global warming The gradual increase in Earth's average temperature

insulate Prevent something from losing energy

insulators Materials that slow or stop electricity moving through them

investigations Procedures carried out to observe, study, or test something in order to learn more about it

magnetic field The invisible area around a magnet or electromagnet in which the force of magnetism acts

microphone A device that uses sound waves to generate an electric current, to transmit or record sound

motors Devices that produce movement using spinning of an electromagnet inside a permanent magnet

neutrons Small parts of an atom that have no electric charge and do not move

nonrenewable resources Substances that cannot be renewed

observe To use your senses to gather information

power lines Cable used to carry current across long distances

power plants Factories where electricity is made

protons Small parts of an atom that have a positive electric charge but do not move

solar panels Devices that can convert light from the Sun into electrical energy

sound waves Vibrations in air that produce noise

source A place, person, or thing from which something originates or can be obtained

turbine A machine with blades that are turned, for example by push of steam, water, or wind, usually to operate a generator

vibration Moving back and forth or shaking

LEARNING MORE

Find out more about electricity and its uses.

Books

Canavan, Thomas. *Excellent Experiments with Electricity and Magnetism* (Mind-Blowing Science Experiments). Gareth Stevens, 2017.

Claybourne, Anna. *Electric Shocks and Other Energy Evils* (Disgusting and Dreadful Science). Crabtree Publishing Company, 2013.

Holzweiss, Kristina. *Amazing Makerspace DIY With Electricity* (True Books). Children's Press, 2017.

Marsico, Katie. *Electricity Investigations* (Key Questions in Physical Science). Lerner Publishing Group, 2017.

Monroe, Ronald. *What Is Electricity?* (Understanding Electricity). Crabtree Publishing Company, 2012.

Websites

There is a lot to learn about energy and electricity at:
www.eia.gov/kids/energy.cfm?page=electricity_home-basics

For a history of electricity and lots of facts and information, visit:
www.explainthatstuff.com/electricity.html

Find out more about how electricity is made, how it gets to your house, and more at:
www.alliantenergykids.com/EnergyBasics/AllAboutElectricity

There are fun facts about electricity and more at:
www.enwin.com/kids/electricity/index.cfm

INDEX

About the AUTHOR

Richard Spilsbury has a science degree, and has had a lifelong fascination with science. He has written and co-written many books for young people on a wide variety of topics, from ants to avalanches.